by **Lauren Thompson** pictures by **Derek Anderson**

Mama Duck had five little ducklings, Widdle, Waddle, Piddle, Puddle and Little Quack.
They all played together in the cool, shady pond.

One day, out jumped a teeny green frog.
"Ribbit, Ribbit! I'm Little Ribbit!" he said. "Can I play?"

"No," said Widdle. "You're too tiny!"
"And you're too green!" said Waddle.
"And you can't quack!" said Piddle.
"And you're a FROG!" said Puddle.
"That's okay!" said Little Quack. "*I* want to play!"

So *quack, quack, ribbit, ribbit!*
– two little friends went off to play.

Over by the reeds, Little Ribbit said, “Let’s splash!”
“I love to splash!” said Little Quack.
Splishy, splosh!
“Can I splash with you?” asked Widdle.

"Of course!" said Little Ribbit.
Splishy, sploshy, splish! splashed three wet friends.

Over in the mud, Little Ribbit said, “Let’s squish!”
“We love to squish!” said Widdle and Little Quack.
Squashy, squooshy, squash!
“Can I squish with you?” asked Waddle.

“Certainly!” said Little Ribbit.
Squashy, squooshy, squashy, squoosh!
squished four muddy friends.

Up on the log, Little Ribbit said, “Let’s bounce!”
“We love to bounce!” said Widdle, Waddle and
Little Quack.
Boingo, poingo, boingo, poing!
“Can I bounce with you?” asked Piddle.

"Why not?" said Little Ribbit.
Boingo, poingo, boingo, boing!
bounced five hoppy friends.

Down by the lily pads, Little Ribbit said,
"Let's dunk!"
"We love to dunk!" said Widdle, Waddle,
Piddle and Little Quack.
Plunka, splunka, plunka, splunka, plunk!
"Can I dunk with you?" asked Puddle.

"Come on over!" said Little Ribbit.
Plunka, splunka, plunka, splunka, plunka, splunk!
dunked six bottoms-up friends.

Then Widdle said to Little Ribbit, "You know what?
It's okay if you're tiny!"
"And it's okay if you're green!" said Waddle.
"And it's okay if you can't quack!" said Piddle.
"And it's okay if you're a FROG!" said Puddle.
"We *all* like to play!" said Little Quack.

Then *splishy, sploshy, squashy, squooshy, poingo, boingo, plunka, splunka!* – how they played!

“Hooray for Little Ribbit,
our *ribbitty* new friend!”

SIMON AND SCHUSTER

First published in Great Britain in 2005 by Simon & Schuster UK Ltd,
Africa House, 64-78 Kingsway, London WC2B 6AH.

Originally published in 2005 by Simon & Schuster Books for Young Readers,
an imprint of Simon & Schuster Children's Publishing Division, New York.

This paperback edition published in 2005.

Book design by Greg Stadnyk.
The text for this book is set in Stine Informal and 99.
The illustrations are rendered in acrylic on canvas.

2 4 6 8 10 9 7 5 3 1

A CIP catalogue record for this book is available from the British Library upon request.

0 689 87522 3
Manufactured in China